TALES OF DOROTHY

A CHURCH MOUSE

Janice B. Scott

Dedicated to the lovely people of St. Andrew's Church, Trowse, Norwich.

I give you a new commandment, that you love one another. Just as I have loved you, you also should love one another. By this everyone will know that you are my disciples, if you have love for one another.

John 13:34-35.

Dorothy, The Harvest Mouse

Dorothy knew she was a little overweight. She didn't much care. When she was a young mouse she'd had to forage for crumbs, so now she ate any scrap that came her way.

Dorothy loved Harvest Festival when the church was festooned with vegetables and fruit of every kind. Mind you, it was better in the old days when everything was fresh. Nowadays folk brought packets and tins, which posed something of a problem for a mouse, especially for Dorothy who was getting on in years. But with a bit of luck that lovely, plaited harvest loaf would be on the high altar, a sheaf of corn would be adorning the choir stalls, and a wheelbarrow full of marrows and apples, potatoes, cabbages and carrots would be standing by the chancel steps. Easy pickings.

Dorothy regarded the church as her own. She had been the only mouse there for years, ever since Herbert had sadly died, chomping his way through a large turnip. Despite his unfortunate and premature demise through over-eating, Dorothy intended to eat her fill at Harvest Festival, and if there was anything she couldn't manage, she would drag it away to her home under the tower and store it there for a rainy day.

On the eve of Harvest Festival Dorothy waited patiently all day, securely concealed in her tiny hole under the tower until all the busy people had finished decorating the church with delicious mouse food. When the coast was clear, she would venture out into the empty church all by herself and eat and eat and eat. She sighed blissfully as she contemplated an evening of unbridled perfection.

But Dorothy had a nasty shock. While the church door had been open, a large tribe of hungry mice had crept stealthily in. All of them were thin and gaunt. All their little black eyes were shining at the sight of so much food and all their little pink noses were quivering.

Dorothy was horrified. These mice were strangers. She didn't know any of them and she certainly didn't like them. Nasty looking creatures, all claws and tails. Why, they didn't even look British! They probably couldn't understand the language either. They had no right to invade Dorothy's territory. This church and all that was in it was hers, all hers. If she let this lot start on the food there was no telling where it might lead. Mice from everywhere might descend, and why should they have any food when they weren't church mice and never darkened the door at any other time? They had no right. And they would ruin the lovely harvest display with their unpleasant little teeth marks. Besides, once they got started, there might be none left for Dorothy herself. She bared her own sharp little

teeth and emitted angry squeaks. Then she fluffed up her fur to make herself as big as possible and scampered as fast as her fat little legs would carry her, charging straight into the ranks of the smelly, tattered tribe of strangers.

The strange mice might be thin, smelly and tattered, but they fought back, and because they were hungry, they fought hard. Clearly they had no notion of a fair fight, for they scratched and bit and clawed and kicked Dorothy in a totally uncaring way until she was so bruised and sore she could hardly stand. She was forced to retreat, slinking away into a dark corner where she lay resentfully licking her wounds and watching as the hungry mice devoured everything they could find. Then as quickly as they had come they vanished, squeezing under the heavy church door and out into the churchyard.

One tiny mouse, slower, smaller and more timid than the rest, stayed behind. He ventured close to Dorothy with some ears of corn tucked between his paws. In a surprise move, he offered the corn to Dorothy.

'I'm sorry. We were hungry,' he explained. 'We only wanted to share - and look, there's plenty left. There was enough for everyone. We would never have hurt you if only you had shared.'

Dorothy looked, and sure enough, most of the harvest food was still there and the displays still looked good, apart from the odd sheaf of corn lying in one of the aisles. Dorothy felt so ashamed. She vowed that in future she would share and share and share again, for she remembered that everything in life is given by God, and if no mice are greedy, there is always plenty for all.

Dorothy Has A Scare

Dorothy settled down on her special patch on the church floor in front of the high altar in the late October sun, washing her whiskers. It was a good spot, because she knew that the sun rising in the East would stream through the great East window all morning. Unless, of course, it rained. Not that Dorothy cared much about the rain since she never ventured out of the church, but she didn't like the cold.

As winter approached Dorothy would pray for plenty of activity in the church, because she knew that if people were there, the heat would be turned on. Without human beings, the church could be a cold and lonely place in winter for a slightly overweight mouse. Dorothy tolerated human beings as long as they didn't get too close. Fortunately they rarely noticed Dorothy, who would squeeze into her tiny hole under the tower as soon as she heard footsteps.

There was one night of the year which Dorothy dreaded, on the very last day of October. Then she always prayed that the church would remain firmly shut and human beings would stay away. She certainly didn't want the church doors left open, because she had heard that dead bodies in the graveyard rise up at Halloween, and that was enough to terrify any self-respecting mouse.

This year Dorothy thought she'd be safe because October 31st fell on a Monday. Nothing much happened in church on a Monday. Sunday was the busy day and people wandered in and out on Thursdays, Fridays and Saturdays to get the church properly prepared for Sunday, but it seemed everyone in the church had a rest on Mondays.

It was a shock then, to hear a scream and a loud bang just as darkness fell. Dorothy had crept towards one of the radiators for the last vestiges of heat following yesterday's Sunday service when to her horror, she saw the church door crash open and two figures stagger through. Clearly Dorothy's prayers were either unheard or unanswered, or both. Dorothy's head lifted, her little pink nose quivered and her whiskers trembled.

There was a huge figure of a skeleton with a grinning skull which made Dorothy's teeth rattle in fear. The smaller figure was a devil, with horns and a tail and gleaming red eyes in a hideous face. Both were covered in blood and the devil was emitting horrible groans.

Was it true, then? Did the dead really rise from their graves on Halloween? Dorothy shivered and shook. She was so terrified she couldn't move. Besides, she was trapped by the radiator. If she scurried across the church floor the two evil creatures would spot her, and that would be the end of Dorothy.

Then Dorothy realised that the little devil was crying. She heard him wail, 'My knee really hurts, Daddy.'

In an unexpectedly normal voice the skeleton replied, 'Let's get this costume with all its fake blood off you, then I'll wash your knee and find a plaster for it. It's only a graze, and there's always a First Aid box in church. You'll be fine.'

Dorothy felt so stupid. It was only a Dad and his son dressed up for a bit of fun, after all.

'I should have remembered tomorrow is All Saints' Day,' Dorothy thought. 'The saints were never so scared that they forgot their faith, and neither should I. All Saints Day is full of light and the promise that God is always with me whatever happens. And I reckon God makes sure the graveyard is as quiet on Halloween as on any other night of the year! Thank you, God.'

And with that, Dorothy rested her little head on her little paws, wrapped her tail firmly around herself and fell fast asleep.

Dorothy's Terror

Dorothy's little pink nose quivered and her whiskers trembled. She was so frightened she just wanted to hide in a corner where no one could spot her, but she couldn't move. There she was, in the middle of the church floor, frozen to the spot.

Crash! Bang! Crash! Strange coloured lights cascaded across the sky outside.

Dorothy hid her head under her paws. She tried to scamper away, but her fat little legs had turned to jelly and refused to move. Dorothy was stuck - and the crashes grew louder and louder and more and more terrifying.

Dorothy shivered and shook. A tiny squeak escaped her.

A voice called, 'What's up, Dorothy? Why did you call me?'

'Call you? I didn't call anyone.' Dorothy's voice remained in the squeak zone but with an added shake. Since no one had ever spoken to her before, she wondered whether it was God, and that was even more terrifying than the bangs and crashes.

'Well, you squeaked high enough to wake all the dead in the churchyard! So here I am to discover what's wrong.'

Dorothy risked raising her head. Her little ears twitched this way and that and her little pink nose sniffed the air, but she couldn't detect anyone.

Crash!

Terrified, Dorothy squeaked again. What enormous, frightful thing could be making that terrible noise? Had the voice come to gobble her up in one juicy mouthful? Was God telling her her time was up?

'Oh, Dorothy!' sighed the unknown voice.

Dorothy forced a squeaky reply. ' I can't see you, God! Am I going to die? Or is something going to eat me?'

'I'm not God,' said the voice, with a hint of laughter. 'Look up.'

Dorothy squinted up. Dangling from a long thread which went right up into the church rafters, was a large, black spider.

Dorothy said, 'Who are you?'

'Surely you remember me? I'm Charlie. When you squeak, I come down to help. I came last year at the same time. I'm your friend, Charlie.'

Dorothy didn't remember. Dorothy thought it was a waste of time and effort to remember anything. Life was about living now. Why bother to remember anything that had happened in the past? That was history and everyone knew history was boring, so Dorothy never made any attempt to remember.

Charlie Spider extended his thread, inching carefully down towards Dorothy.

'Oh, Dorothy!' he sighed again. 'History matters. You need to remember so that you can stop awful things happening again. Take these bangs and the coloured lights, for instance. They're fireworks and they won't harm you at all. Humans use them to remind them of a time when their parliament - it rules the country - was nearly blown up. They don't want that to happen again, so they remember it each year on November 5th. That's today. If you had remembered that, Dorothy, you wouldn't be so terrified now. The bangs and flashes can't hurt you. They're just entertainment for human beings.'

Dorothy was intrigued. History could be useful? Really? That was a new thought.

'What else do humans remember?' she asked.

Charlie said, 'November is a remembering month. They remember some terrible wars and the people who fought and died. That's a really important memory, because maybe, just maybe, it makes human beings think before embarking upon war again. War kills and injures so many people. Wars make everyone really sad.'

Dorothy thought about that. She wondered whether that was why humans came to church every Sunday, to remember the life and death of Jesus and how he was still able to set folk free from all that worried and disturbed them.

Then she shook her head. Such thoughts were much too deep for a little fat mouse. She cleaned her whiskers and laid her head on her paws, but just before nodding off she vowed that in future she would always remember her friend, Charlie.

Dorothy Is Lonely

Dorothy felt so sad that she thought she might weep. If only a slightly overweight mouse could shed tears! She also felt guilty about feeling sad because everybody knows Christmas is the happiest time of the whole year, so what right did a fat little mouse have to feel sad?

Normally Dorothy loved it when the church was full of people. She would watch from her little home under the floor of the tower enjoying the hustle and bustle and excited cries of the children. Usually she especially loved Christmas, when the church was full of flowers and lights and decorations and had at least one Christmas tree which promised rich pickings for a mouse. A chocolate ornament or a stray biscuit decoration could be guaranteed to fall off. Dorothy would be ready when it did.

But on Christmas Eve this year Dorothy was suddenly aware of being alone. She had nobody with whom to share the excitement of Christmas. Human beings were with family and friends, but there were no other mice in the church - Dorothy had made sure of that since she considered it her own territory - and now Dorothy felt desperately lonely. There was no one to care for her. In fact, human beings quite often screamed if ever they caught sight of her, and placed nasty, sneaky traps filled with tempting cheese in order to catch and execute her.

Dorothy felt so lonely that after the Christingle service when everyone was drinking mulled wine and eating mince pies, she dared to venture out from her hole under the tower even though she was afraid someone might see her or accidentally tread on her. Her little pink nose twitched and her whiskers quivered as she crept forward, feeling an overwhelming need to be with company. But they were all so busy eating and drinking and laughing and having fun that nobody noticed her standing there all alone. Dorothy emitted a tiny squeak, but nobody heard her. She felt depressed. She knew no one would ever leave any human being alone at Christmas, but they didn't care about a slightly overweight mouse.

Sadly, she crept towards the Christmas crib. Perhaps she could burrow under the straw to be close to the baby Jesus. Of course she knew the baby in the crib was just a doll, but somehow she thought she might be nearer to God if she was close to the baby. Even if she could never see God, it was a comfort to know God was there and cared even for elderly, overweight mice.

Silently Dorothy inched her way over to the crib. As she was about to snuggle under the straw, she was sure she saw baby Jesus wink. Of course, she knew she couldn't possibly have done so in real life, for baby Jesus was just a doll, but it was a comfort nonetheless, and the next best thing to reality.

 At that very moment Dorothy spotted a small boy staring at her. Dorothy was terri-fied. Now the child would scream and everyone would be upset and worse, fetch out that hideous trap and try to capture her. But to Dorothy's surprise the boy stood quite still. He and Dorothy stared at each other. Then the boy quietly placed his half eaten mince pie on the straw, and Dorothy knew instinctively it was for her. Her very own Christmas dinner.

What a gift for a lonely little mouse! Dorothy was overwhelmed by the love behind the gift and suddenly realised what Christmas was about - the gift of love from God to his people. With that thought and the lovely gift of Christmas dinner, Dorothy's loneliness vanished. God loved her and somebody cared, and that was all that mat-tered.

Dorothy's Resolutions

Christmas was over, although in church it always seemed to last for a lot longer than in the world outside. But even in church things had quietened down considerably since Christmas Day. The Christmas trees, the decorations and the sparkly lights remained for a few more days, but the only excitement now was that of a brand new year.

Not that a New Year meant much to Dorothy. To her it felt much the same as the Old Year, except that she was aware of the passage of time through new creaks and groans in her fat little body, always worse in the cold of winter.

'You should exercise more,' Charlie had informed her. 'That will keep you supple, and warm you up as well.'

And since Charlie knew everything, Dorothy supposed he must be right. Consequently she embarked upon a number of New Year Resolutions. It was unfortunate that she was unable to write (you can't hold a pen in mouse paws) because it meant entrusting the resolutions to memory, and Dorothy only possessed the memory span of a goldfish. She contemplated reciting her resolutions to Charlie who certainly would remember them, but that felt like a step too far. Dorothy was uneasily aware that she might not care to be reminded of her resolutions in say, June or July.

Still, it was only the beginning of January, so worth embarking upon them right now.

'I want to be different,' Dorothy thought. 'I want to be much slimmer, and I want to think of things other than food. I'd like to be clever too, like Charlie, but that might prove to be impossible. I want to be less selfish and more generous. In fact, I want a complete makeover into an entirely new, slimline, energetic, kind, generous, unselfish, lovely mouse.'

It sounded good, even though she had little idea where or how to start. In the end, she whittled it down to two resolutions, which was about all her tiny mouse brain could hack. She resolved to eat less and be nicer.

Dorothy's resolutions lasted for all of ten minutes, until she spotted a clump of discarded mince pie crumbs, which had somehow been missed by the Hoover. Without a second thought, Dorothy sped over to the crumbs as fast as her fat little legs would carry her and wolfed down the crumbs like there was no tomorrow.

This was immediately followed by heavy feelings of guilt, which she managed to assuage by reminding herself that in winter food was scarce for a little elderly mouse, and she needed all the sustenance she could get whenever she could get it. But she still felt like a failure.

'I can't do anything,' she moaned to herself, 'so why bother to try? New Year Resolutions are stupid anyway.'

As though he had heard her thoughts, Charle slid down his silken thread from the rafters. 'Dorothy,' he said sternly, 'put away those negative thoughts. You know you are special in God's eyes. God sees you exactly as you are, not as you have been or how you could be, and God still loves you with an overwhelming love. You know all that, deep down inside. And you must also know that it's impossible to change yourself. No one can do that. What you can do—if you really want to change—is ask God to help you. Then you'll find that you begin to change without even realising it. Or more to the point, other people —like me—will notice the change in you. So come on. Just be yourself. That's all you need to do.'

Dorothy pondered Charlie's words and felt better. It was so much easier just to be herself. She padded over to her special spot on the church floor, barely warmed in the watery January sunshine, but with the definite promise of better times to come.

Dorothy Feels Miserable

Dorothy's little pink nose twitched and her whiskers quivered. She wasn't sure what she wanted. Was she looking for something or waiting for someone? Dorothy was rarely certain of her memory, but she always knew about her feelings. She knew too that in every February she felt the same. Cold, of course, and a bit miserable, which she blamed on the month. With those thick stone walls from the fifteenth century, the inside of the church was probably several degrees colder than outside, and certainly colder than a little overweight mouse could stand.

Dorothy shivered. She thought of her distant cousins the dormice (whom she had never met but that was beside the point) who boasted about sleeping through the whole winter, and she sighed. It was alright for them. Cuddled up in their beds of straw, they never knew what it was to be cold. Even her closest relatives, the house mice, sank into a state of torpor in the very coldest weather, but church mice were such a special breed that they couldn't afford to spend months in a coma. As a church mouse, Dorothy had work to do. She knew she was in charge of the church, nibbling up all the tiny bits and pieces human folk dropped after coffee and cake at the end of the Sunday service. It was an important job, even though the humans fondly believed they achieved the clean floors with the Hoover. Ha! What did they know? So although Dorothy was bitterly cold, that wasn't the whole problem. There was something more, but what?

Then, in a flash of insight, Dorothy recalled Herbert. She wasn't sure how long Herbert had been with her or how long he had been gone, but she did remember that awful moment one February when he was chomping through an overlarge turnip and suddenly keeled over. His eyes always had been bigger than his belly. Dorothy never saw him again, since with a shriek one of the humans spotted his dead body, swept him up in a dustpan and deposited him in the bin. There was no funeral for Herbert. One minute he was there, large as life itself, the next he was gone, never to be seen again. It was harsh.

Dorothy suddenly missed Herbert so much that she felt like weeping all over again, if only a little overweight mouse could weep. She felt there was no future for her all alone, even though she had managed alone for quite some time. But in the cold bleakness of an empty church in February, there didn't seem much to look forward to.

Dorothy muttered a little prayer for help not expecting much in the way of results, but just at that moment a ray of winter sunshine shone through the window straight onto Dorothy. Suddenly she felt warm and contented and loved all at the same time.

'Thank you, God,' Dorothy murmured, and then she remembered something quite astonishing for a little overweight mouse. As well as being a cold and miserable month, February heralded the approach of Spring, and God had made the 14th a special day - St. Valentine's Day - for everyone to know they are loved. Dorothy didn't expect a Valentine's card (although a few tasty crumbs wouldn't go amiss) but she was quite certain that everyone, even a lonely, cold, overweight mouse, was thoroughly, totally and utterly loved by God.

It Must Be Something To Do With Spring.

'It must be something to do with Spring,' Dorothy thought as she hesitated by the big, oak door, her little pink nose twitching and her whiskers quivering. She so wanted to go out, to venture forth into the great wide world out there and to be part of it, but she was scared.

Dorothy couldn't remember ever going outside the church. She thought she must have been born in the church and she had a very hazy memory of a warm nest and the furry body of someone she thought must have been her mother. But that was aeons ago. Dorothy had no idea how long ago because she didn't know how old she was, but she worried sometimes that she was slowly becoming ancient. She was aware that her fat little legs didn't always react as quickly as she thought they should and that was a scary thought, because a mouse that can't scamper away at the first sign of danger is a mouse who will almost certainly get caught.

'If I really am growing old,' Dorothy thought, 'I should do now everything I want to do, before it's too late.'

Then she thought that the only thing she had ever really wanted to do was to go outside into the churchyard. So why not? Why shouldn't she go out?

'Ah,' said that uncomfortable warning voice in Dorothy's head, 'If you go out, will you be able to get back in again? Now that strip of draught excluder is at the bottom of the big oak door and you're somewhat overweight, will you be able to squeeze under if the door is shut? It's a terrible risk, and for what? You know what it's like outside. You've seen it when the door has been opened. Why would you want to risk it? Besides, if you do it once, you might want to do it again and again and again, and then you'd be a field mouse or a dormouse or something, not a really special and nearly unique church mouse.'

Perhaps it was better to stay where she was, warm and snug in the church. Well, mostly warm and snug, except in winter when it was perishing cold most of the time apart from those rare occasions when the heat was on. About once a week. Maybe at those times it would be warmer outside. Oh dear! What a dilemma. To venture forth into pastures new, or to stay where she knew it was safe and secure and familiar. Perhaps at her age it was a mistake to even think of trying anything new. Perhaps she should just settle down into old age and be content with what she had.

Then, with a sudden insight and another well-worn cliché she thought, 'Nothing ventured, nothing gained.' And the next time the big oak door opened, Dorothy took a deep breath, squeezed her eyes shut and darted through.

When she opened her eyes out in the big wide world—or the churchyard at any rate —it was a revelation. Although she had seen outside on numerous occasions, nothing could have prepared Dorothy for what it was really like. The feel of the sun on her back. The scent of the spring flowers. The brilliance of the sky and the myriad different colours. The freshness, the breeze, the newness of it all. For a moment Dorothy stood there mesmerised, absorbing, amazed and enjoying this new experience.

Then she turned and quickly slipped back into her home before the big oak door had a chance to close.

'Thank you, God,' breathed Dorothy. 'Thank you for showing me it's always worth the effort. And thank you for reminding me that as long as I have life I'll never be too old to try new things, because that's what life is about. Going forward, trusting in you, and knowing that you'll never let me down.'

And with that Dorothy curled up in her tiny hole under the tower, rested her little head on her little grey paws, and fell fast asleep, as befits an almost elderly, slightly overweight church mouse.

Easter Lilies

'Oh dear, oh dear, oh dear,' muttered Charlie as he slowly unwound himself from the rafters on a long silken thread. 'Oh dear.'

'Whatever's the matter?' Dorothy was cross. Having just found herself a patch of warm sunlight on the church floor where she could curl up and doze quietly as befitted a slightly overweight mouse of advancing years, she had no wish to be disturbed.

Charlie descended as low as he dared. 'It's the Easter lilies.'

'The Easter lilies? What on earth are you talking about now?'

'Well, there won't be any, will there?'

'Won't be any?'

It was Charlie's turn to feel cross. 'I do wish you'd listen instead of repeating everything I say! Easter is so late this year - almost the latest it can ever be - so the Easter lilies will be over, won't they?'

Dorothy sighed, any thoughts of a comfortable snooze having vanished. She pushed herself up on her fat little legs and her little pink nose twitched. 'Don't be silly. We always have gorgeous white lilies for Easter. It's nothing to do with how late Easter is because they come from abroad. I think,' she added, doubtfully. 'At any rate, I've heard that head flower lady saying how expensive they are and I'm pretty sure people in church help out with the cost.'

Charlie snorted, not easy for a spider with eight legs and a body and not much else. 'I don't mean those, silly! Of course they'll be there. I mean the daffodils. You know, the yellow ones with the trumpets.'

'I know what daffodils are and they're not Easter lilies,' Dorothy said indignantly, 'they're just daffodils. Why are you calling them Easter lilies?'

Charlie spoke very slowly and clearly as if to a five-year old instead of a slightly overweight mouse of advancing years. 'The old English name for a daffodil was 'Easter lily' because daffodils were the first long stemmed flowers to come out in the Spring. You couldn't buy flowers from abroad in those days, so at Easter the church was filled with golden daffodils. They represent the resurrection, see.'

Dorothy didn't quite see but she wasn't about to admit it. 'Oh yes!'

'Yes indeed! Jesus died on Good Friday and his body was put in this dark, gloomy cave and left there all Saturday because that was a holy day for Jews and no one was allowed to work on Saturdays. Then on the next day, Sunday, the women went to the cave early on because they had to lay out the body - wash it and put on special oils and stuff like that - only it wasn't there. Jesus had risen and was alive again.'

'Yes, I know all that,' Dorothy said impatiently. 'Everyone knows that. But what has it got to do with daffodils? Or with chocolate eggs and bunnies and baby chicks, come to that?'

Charlie sighed. 'You still don't get it? They all represent new life. Chocolate eggs always used to be hollow representing the dark cave, and when you opened them there was nothing inside, just like Jesus and his tomb. Baby bunnies and chicks are born in Spring, the first new life of the year, and the glorious yellow of daffodils comes first of all the main flowers after a cold, dark winter. In Spring, new life is all around us and that's what resurrection is all about. New life.'

'Oh!' said Dorothy, faintly and her whiskers quivered as she settled down in her patch of sunlight and firmly closed her eyes. There was only so much brain work a little fat mouse could manage in one day.

Dorothy Wants To Ascend

Dorothy was feeling quite frisky. Well, as frisky as a somewhat elderly mouse can feel. Charlie Spider (who knew everything) had told her it was because of Spring, but Dorothy knew it was because of a lean winter. She couldn't feel much spring in her fat little legs, just enough to skitter across the church floor if anyone approached.

That was the trouble with growing old, Dorothy decided. The spring in your legs became autumn almost without you noticing, and autumn in America was aptly named The Fall. Not that Dorothy had far to fall since these days she was wary about climbing onto anything higher than a hassock. Unfortunately, since hardly anyone knelt in church any more, there were very few hassocks about, so Dorothy was mostly restricted to the floor.

Still, she was frisky in her mind if not in her body, and there were plenty of events going on in church these days which involved food. Food, Dorothy had noticed, was often dropped by human beings, and therefore made easy pickings for a hungry little mouse with fat little legs. Easter had been especially tasty with hot cross bun crumbs on Good Friday after the service, and nibbles of chocolate here and there after the Easter Day service. Then there was an unexpected addition for a hungry little mouse - a bring and share lunch on the Sunday after Easter where everybody brought loads of food and there was plenty left over. There were lots of crumbs after that. Dorothy spent a happy afternoon hoovering as many crumbs as she could, cramming them into her mouth.

There was only one problem. Too many crumbs made a fat little mouse fatter still, so Dorothy found herself puffing and panting in an effort to climb onto one of the few remaining hassocks, only to fall back to the floor again and again. Perhaps she should wait until the end of the month. Dorothy had heard some mention of 'Ascension Day', so presumably that was a good day to ascend.

She mentioned her idea to Charlie who was hanging about as usual on the end of a long silken thread attached to the rafters, but was deeply offended when Charlie shook so much with laughter that he was in danger of falling to the floor.

"Don't ask me to pick you up when you fall,' Dorothy huffed crossly. 'You wait till you're old and can't climb up your silly rope again. Then you'll know what it feels like.' And she turned her back with a flounce.

'Sorry,' gasped Charlie, wiping tears from his eyes with one of his eight legs. 'I didn't mean to upset you. It's just that after Jesus ascended on Ascension Day, he never came to earth again.'

'You mean he didn't just climb a mountain somewhere?' Dorothy was intrigued despite herself. 'Isn't that what 'ascension' means? To climb higher?'

Charlie swallowed more laughter. 'Er, no, not exactly. Well, I suppose it does mean that, but it wasn't quite like that for Jesus. He ascended right enough, but went all the way to Heaven and now lives in Heaven.'

'What do you mean, he lives in Heaven? Only dead people go to Heaven don't they?'

"Not really. People do die on this earth, but in Heaven they're alive again in a different sort of way. That was what Jesus showed us. He died on that awful cross, but after Easter Day he was seen again alive for about six weeks, although he wasn't quite the same. He could walk through locked doors and be in two places at the same time, and nobody really recognised him.'

Dorothy frowned. 'Like a ghost, do you mean?'

'Well, no. He was real enough, to show us that death isn't the end. Life goes on, but it's a bit different and in a different sphere. People used to think that Heaven was above the sky and that's why Jesus went upwards - ascended. Nowadays we're not so sure that Heaven is 'up there.' It could be anywhere, all around us maybe.'

'So Ascension Day won't help me climb up onto any of the hassocks?"

Charlie shook his head. 'I'm afraid not. But the good news is, if you don't eat any crumbs for a month you'll soon get up on those hassocks again!' And with that, he scrambled back up his silken thread, chortling with laughter.

Dorothy narrowed her eyes and glared at his retreating back. Then she curled up in a patch of sunlight on the church floor, twitched her little pink nose, laid her head on her little brown paws, and slept.

What's An Election?

'What's an election?' Dorothy asked plaintively. 'Everyone's talking about an election, but I don't know what that is.'

Charlie sighed. It was a long journey from the rafters just to answer stupid questions. 'It's when people go to a special place and write an X on a piece of paper against the name of the person they wish to vote for. If that person gets the most votes, he or she becomes a Member of Parliament. The party with the most Members of Parliament gets to govern the country.'

Dorothy's little bright eyes had glazed over during this explanation, but at the word 'party' she perked up.

'I love parties. Where is the party? Can anyone go?'

Charlie wanted to grind his teeth at such ignorance, but as he was devoid of teeth had to be content with grinding a couple of his eight legs together.

'There's no need to be like that,' Dorothy retorted sharply. 'Anyway, what happens to your vote if the person you voted for doesn't get the most votes?'

Charlie frowned. 'Why, nothing, of course. Your fella just didn't win, so that's it.'

'So if my fella didn't win, does that mean I just don't get any say over anything?'

'It's like a race,' Charlie explained patiently, suppressing a loud sigh. 'The first person past the post wins, and that's it.'

Dorothy wasn't finished. 'But there's usually a second and a third prize in a race, isn't there?'

'Well, sorry,' Charlie said. 'There isn't in politics in this country. I'm afraid if your fella doesn't win, that's it. Tough luck.'

Dorothy shook her head. 'I'll never understand humans. They're a weird bunch. Anyway, I live in a church so I'd like to know what any of this has to do with the church?'

'Nothing really. Human beings aren't allowed to mix religion and politics. If they ever do, there's a terrible explosion and people get hurt—well, not hurt physically—hurt inside themselves, because human beings hate disagreements. They can't cope with them. But church people are expected to vote for the political party they think will deliver the best outcome for the most people, because that's what they care about. They want the best for everyone, not just for themselves.'

'So that the government increases the money it gives to maintain the church?'

Charlie laughed. 'You really don't know anything, do you? The government doesn't give a single penny to maintain the church. The people themselves have to pay to keep this building - your home and mine - in good repair.'

Now Dorothy was really confused. 'But it's called a state church, isn't it? And this building is huge and you told me it's something like 700 years old. It must cost a fortune to keep it going.'

'None of that matters. It still has to be paid for by the people, not the government.'

Dorothy twitched her whiskers. 'In that case, if it's no advantage to anyone here, why would they bother to vote?'

'Ah,' said Charlie, 'that's just how the wrong party can get into government, because people are so fed up with it all they can't be bothered to vote, specially if they think their fella has no chance of winning. If it's been someone from the same party in their area (it's called a constituency, by the way) for ever and ever, they can't see the point of voting because they know nothing is going to change. But if everyone in the country had to vote by law, it might be a very different outcome.'

Dorothy yawned. The ways of human beings were difficult to fathom for an elderly little mouse. And Charlie could be so boring when he started to lecture. She scurried away on her fat little legs without even a 'Goodbye' or 'Thank you' to Charlie, and settled down to sleep in a patch of sunlight on the church floor, glad that she didn't have to vote.

Charlie shrugged. He was used to Dorothy and he never bore a grudge. He ran back up his silken thread to his home in the rafters. He didn't much care what happened in elections, but he did wonder for a moment what God thought about it all.

Dorothy's Holiday

It was a long time since Dorothy had been on holiday. In fact, never. She had only been outside the church on one occasion, and that was quite recently. Even then, she had just twitched her nose outside the great main door, cautiously sniffed the air (marvelling at how different fresh air smelled outside the church from the air inside, even when the door was open), wondered at the brightness and the fresh colours of the Spring flowers in the churchyard, and scurried back inside with her heart beating wildly.

It wasn't that she was afraid, of course not! But to a fat little mouse getting on in years, the outside was terrifyingly big and scary. Perhaps if she had been able to venture forth to explore the churchyard while she was still young, she might have been all right, but now she felt time had passed her by. She was better off with what she knew and loved—her little home under the tower and her patch on sunlight on the church floor.

But somehow, that one glimpse of the great wide world outside the church had made Dorothy restless. From time to time she'd had visits from her country cousins, who had told her such tales of faraway cities, wondrous treasures, and animals Dorothy couldn't even begin to imagine. Mostly she had dismissed the stories as wild exaggeration because she knew the country cousins quite envied her, a church mouse, especially in winter when it was so cold outside. And she'd never let them know it was equally cold inside the church, since she was inordinately proud of being unique, a church mouse all her life.

Now though, it wasn't cold. Summer had arrived. The sun was shining, the sky was a cloudless bright blue, and it seemed as if the outside world was beckoning. Perhaps, just this once, she could make a brief visit to the country cousins. It wouldn't be long since the church probably couldn't function at all without Dorothy, but maybe… just maybe…

Dorothy fetched her little suitcase and packed her tiny bikini. She'd had it for years but never actually worn it on account that she'd never been away. She wasn't at all sure it would still fit her, since she hadn't found much opportunity to wear a bikini in church. Then she packed the food, since obviously a little fat mouse can't travel far without a goodly supply of nourishment, and settled in a patch of sunlight by the door, waiting for it to open.

Charlie lowered himself quietly from the rafters on his long silken thread and watched her with a tolerant expression on his face. He chuckled to himself. He knew exactly what would happen, since he'd seen it many times before. Sure enough, within a couple of seconds gentle snores arose from the floor.

The door opened and closed several times as people came and went, but Dorothy still slept on. When she eventually awoke, it was quite dark. She collected up her bikini and her bag of nourishment and scurried happily back to her little home under the tower, her head full of wonderful dreams of sea and sand, wood and meadow, cities, wondrous treasures, and strange animals.

Charlie nodded to himself. He knew his dear friend had had her holiday. It's so good to dream, he thought, sometimes dreams are better than reality because in dreams there is always hope.

'So lovely dreams must be sent from God,' Charlie mused, 'because no matter what the circumstances, even if things are awful, or even if we fail and fail again (like Dorothy trying to go on holiday) God always offers hope.'

Is It Worth The Risk?

Dorothy could hardly contain her excitement. She hopped about from one leg to the other (and with four legs that took a while) but it still didn't quieten her. So she spun around in a few circles and danced a crazy little jig.

It would soon be Open Churches Week! That might not sound like much to cause such major excitement, but Dorothy knew there was to be a Colman's exhibition during each day and a concert on the Friday evening, and all of that added up to PEOPLE! In Dorothy's experience (admittedly limited to church but a long experience nonetheless) people meant food, and food meant crumbs for a hungry, fat little mouse.

Dorothy polished her whiskers and licked her lips in anticipation. Not just one day, but a whole week of the church being open and serving refreshments! The thought of a feast of cake crumbs every day made Dorothy's eyes water.

Dorothy made her plans. At any quiet times during the day she would creep out of her hole, collect as many crumbs as she could manage, and drag them back into her little home under the tower. But she knew the very best pickings would be at the end of each day. Then she would have to time her outing until just after the main doors were closed for the day but just before the Hoover was taken out of its cupboard. Once the Hoover began its relentless task of cleaning the carpets, all crumbs would be quickly absorbed into its dust bag and there would be nothing left at all.

There was just one snag. Lots of people could be dangerous for a little fat mouse. For some reason, if she was ever spotted, human beings would emit piercing shrieks and all sorts of unpleasant things followed, like traps temptingly primed with cheese, or mean, lean cats on the prowl. Even if she wasn't spotted, there was the danger of being trampled under large, human feet. Neither possibility was a pleasant end for a fat little mouse.

Dorothy rested her head on her paws in her patch of sunlight on the church floor and thought. Was it worth the risk? Would it be better to stay in her home out of harm's way? After all, she was getting older. She wasn't quite as sprightly as she had been in her youth. If nobody knew she existed, she couldn't get hurt. Maybe sometimes it was better to keep her head down rather than daring to venture forth. That way she would certainly stay alive, even if hungry.

Then some words she had heard in church sprang into Dorothy's mind. Something about those who lost their life would find it, while those who clung onto their life would lose it. It had never made much sense to Dorothy, but suddenly she thought perhaps she understood. Maybe it was all about daring to take risks!

Dorothy made up her mind. In Open Churches Week she would find her crumbs.

So if you see a fat little mouse when you come into church that week, don't shriek. Just drop a few surreptitious crumbs and walk away.

Where is Charlie?

Dorothy was worried. She hadn't seen Charlie for ages, even though she often scurried on her fat little legs to her patch of sunlight on the church floor, and gazed longingly towards the roof.

It had been a fairly tempestuous time in the church for a somewhat elderly mouse, with lots of comings and goings. Dorothy wondered whether all the activity had frightened Charlie so much that he had clung to his web in the rafters and might never appear again. That made Dorothy really sad, as she had no other friends.

First, there had been the replacement of the huge picture which hung on the south wall of the church. That had meant all the chairs being moved and scaffolding brought in, and people climbing up and down all day. Dorothy herself had stayed under cover while that went on.

Then there had been Open Churches Week. That wasn't so bad, especially as there were always crumbs available. People had come and gone meandering around the church and looking at the Colman's Exhibition of old Trowse, and Dorothy had long since discovered that no human being is capable of eating a biscuit without dropping crumbs. She made sure she was around for the pickings, but again there had been no sign of Charlie.

Now the long summer was almost over, for Dorothy had heard many mutterings of 'Back to School' for several weeks now, but where was Charlie? Had something happened to him?

Dorothy felt so alone the there was only one thing to do. 'Come on God,' she whispered, in a squeaky mouse prayer, 'I'm so lonely. Please help me!'

Then she sighed and lay down in her patch of sunlight on the church floor, not expecting any response from God, for why would God bother to answer the prayer of an elderly overweight mouse who was just feeling sorry for herself?

She must have slept for a while, for when she opened her eyes again there was a long silken thread dangling just above her nose. "Charlie!' Dorothy cried in delight, almost in tears at the sight of her friend again. 'Where have you been? I've missed you so much!'

Then she had the biggest surprise of her life, for clinging to the thread in a line be-hind Charlie were twenty-four tiny spiders. "Charlie?' Dorothy's little pink nose wrin-kled and her whiskers twitched. 'How in the world -?"

Charlie grinned. 'My name certainly is Charlie, but I've always been a her, not a him! You never noticed, so I didn't bother to disillusion you. I must admit,' she added, 'it's difficult to differentiate a her spider from a him spider. But I'm definitely a her, and always have been. These are my new children, born in our home up in the rafters. That's why I've been away for a while. Come children,' she ordered, 'meet my best friend in the whole world, Dorothy the church mouse.'

Dorothy was so happy she thought she might burst. Twenty-four new friends! And Dorothy had a feeling that if God was looking down at her, God would surely have winked.

Things Aren't Always As They Seem

Dorothy huddled in her little home under the tower. She turned round and round in the nest trying to get comfortable, but it was no use. She had been here far too long, but she was afraid to emerge. Dorothy had seen something in the church which terrified her.

It wasn't so long ago that Dorothy had been bemoaning the lack of friends, mostly because she hadn't seen her best (and only) friend Charlie for ages. Then a miracle had happened. Charlie had reappeared with a great brood of twenty-four spider children. Dorothy had been delighted. Twenty-four new friends! Better than she could ever have imagined.

But reality wasn't so good. The trouble was, those tiny spiders were everywhere. They danced on the chairs, they spun webs across any two adjacent surfaces until the whole church seemed to Dorothy to be festooned in spiders' webs, and they were never still. If Dorothy lay down in her patch of sunlight for a quiet snooze, they were more than likely to spin a web between her whiskers.

Charlie seemed unfazed. In fact, Charlie seemed to take no notice at all of the antics of her offspring. She let them get on with whatever they were doing, and never corrected them. She seemed to be of the opinion that if you let children just be themselves and do whatever they want to do, they would grow up fine. It was all very trying for a little elderly mouse, especially when she was trying to sleep.

But the worst thing was that one day she had woken to a nightmare. As she opened her eyes from her nap on the church floor, there was a row of small spiders teasing her and poking her and laughing at her and scrambling all over her fur. That was bad enough, but behind them was a huge black spider, the size of a dinner plate.

Dorothy shuddered. She loved Charlie, but that massive spider-stranger was terrifying. She pushed her way blindly through the row of giggling spider-children and scurried back to her home under the tower as fast as her fat little legs would carry her, her heart thumping.

And there she stayed, for day after day, until there was a gentle knock at her door. A gravelly voice asked politely, 'Miss Dorothy, may I be your friend?'

'Who are you?' Dorothy's voice was high and squeaky with fear.

'Hercules. I'm the oldest and biggest of my mother Charlie's children, but they leave me out because i'm so big. They think I'm a freak, just because I'm different.'

Dorothy blinked. Her heart suddenly melted, for she knew what it was to be rejected and have folk frightened of you for no good reason.

'Hercules,' she said. 'That's a good name. Why, you're not scary at all. You may be huge, but really you're just a big softie. Yes, I'd love to be your friend.'

'Strange,' she mused as she crept out to shake paws with one of Hercules' eight legs, 'how things aren't always as they seem.'

Dorothy Delights In November

Although Dorothy hated the cold and dreaded the onset of winter, she had a sneaking delight in November. Previously she had been terrified of November because of all the loud bangs and the flashing lights around the fifth of the month, but since last year when Charlie had told her all about Guy Fawkes and the Gunpowder Plot, Dorothy's fear had abated. As a mouse of very little brain Dorothy had the memory and attention span of a goldfish, but she had remembered Fireworks Day.

Her unexpected pleasure in November was because almost all the humans who usually attended the church had returned from their various holidays. Dorothy loved the sunshine and warmth of summer and the different events that took place inside the church, but she felt unsettled when familiar faces were absent. It was as though part of her own family was missing, but November heralded the return of many of the holidaymakers, so that Dorothy felt secure and safe again.

The past summer had been particularly unsettling for Dorothy. Her little pink ears were sharp despite their miniscule size, and very often this past summer they had been assaulted by a terrible screech which often occurred in the early hours of the morning just as the sun was rising, when all good mice should be fast asleep. It was always followed by a human briefly arriving, entering the vestry, doing something unknown, then departing again. But a few days later the same strange phenomenon would happen again. And again, and again. It was very disturbing, and Dorothy was exhausted through lack of sleep.

Dorothy wanted to ask Charlie what was happening, but Charlie was so busy with her brood of spider children that Dorothy hadn't wanted to impose. Now, though, the spider children were almost grown up (and not quite so infuriating now they were a little older and wiser) and Charlie had reappeared on her silken thread.

'My family have all made their own webs in the rafters,' Charlie explained in a satisfied voice, 'but after the winter, they'll be off. They have all assured me they have no wish to be stuck in a church for the rest of their lives, like me. All except Hercules, that is. That big boy is a real domesticated spider. I don't think he'll ever leave home.'

Dorothy smiled politely. She didn't want to interrupt, but she was itching to find out about the horrible screeches. 'Um, Charlie?'

Charlie was quite ready to chat, after a whole summer devoted entirely to her children. "Yes?"

'Did you hear that terrible, shrieking noise in the summer, when the sun came up?'

'Did I! It was right above my head! Every time it happened, it disturbed my babies all over again, until the human shut it off.'

'Oh! Is that what the human was doing? What was the noise? I was so scared.'

Charlie said, 'You didn't need to be frightened. They've put an alarm on the roof, because in lots of churches thieves are stripping the lead from the roof. Lead is valuable. It can be sold for money, so the people here have had a roof alarm installed to prevent theft. The trouble is, it's been going off at sunrise—three or four o'clock in the morning—when the birds awake and saunter across the roof. That's set off the alarm, and a human has to come each time to reset it.'

Dorothy thought for a moment. 'You mean, there were no thieves? It was just birds?'

Charlie nodded. 'But I think it's fixed properly now. The humans weren't pleased at getting woken up at that unearthly hour several times a week. But I haven't heard it for a few weeks, so it must be fixed. The humans haven't had to come and reset it since the beginning of Autumn. But it will definitely go off if anyone tries to steal the lead.'

'Hm,' said Dorothy, thoughtfully. 'I suppose it's worth being disturbed to keep our roof intact. I wouldn't like the rain coming in. I just wish birds didn't get up so early.'

And with that she laid her head on her little paws and fell fast asleep.

Dorothy's Christmas Disgrace

Just when she was so cold that she thought she might freeze if ever she stirred from her little home under the tower, Dorothy the church mouse lifted her head, her whiskers quivering. It was utterly silent. Of course, it was often silent in church when there were no people around, but this was different. It was as though a blanket had been dropped over the entire world. Dorothy crept fearfully out into the church. What was going on?

'That's more less exactly what's happened,' Charlie explained, letting herself down on her silken thread until she was hanging just above Dorothy's right ear. 'It's snowing.'

Fortunately, Charlie Spider knew everything.

'Snowing?' asked Dorothy, who had only been outside the church on one brief occasion, back in the Spring. 'What's snow?'

'It comes from the sky. It's very beautiful and it wraps the earth in a white mantle. It's like a blanket for the tiny seeds and shoots. It keeps them safe from the coldest winter nights.'

'Oh!' Dorothy, a mouse of very little brain, pondered this for a long moment until Charlie got fed up with waiting and climbed back up her silken thread into the rafters.

Dorothy wandered over to the Christmas crib to gaze at the baby Jesus lying there. She had often thought how cold he looked. Indeed, on occasion she had clambered up into the crib and nestled down in the straw next to baby Jesus to keep him warm, until human voices had caused her to scuttle away as fast as her fat little legs would carry her.

Suddenly, Dorothy had a brilliant idea. Suddenly, she knew just how to keep the baby warm. She scampered back to the big west door of the church, and holding her breath squeezed underneath through the tiny gap where the draught excluders failed and the draught came swirling in. Tentatively she stepped outside for it was still difficult for her to leave the safety of the church, but then she caught her breath in wonder at the beauty of the churchyard under its blanket of snow. As quickly as she could, Dorothy filled her little paws with snow and carried it back to the crib, where she packed it gently around the sleeping baby. It took many trips as her paws didn't carry much and the snow was colder than anything she had ever experienced before, but at last baby Jesus had his very own beautiful, warm blanket of snow. Dorothy settled down behind a convenient hassock to rest after all her exertions, which had taken their toll on a little, elderly mouse.

***

'Aagh! Look! The crib's soaking wet!' A disgusted voice woke Dorothy. She crept out to see what all the fuss was about, and to her horror saw that baby Jesus was floating in water.

'I think I forget to tell you,' whispered Charlie, who had woven a small web just above the crib to keep an eye on the baby, 'that snow melts into water when it heats. The church heating started four hours ago, ready for the Christmas services.'

Dorothy covered her ears in shame. She had so wanted to help the baby, but all she had done was drown him. Fat tears rolled down her little mouse cheeks, until a child's clear voice made her whiskers quiver.

'Look Mummy, look! Look at that jewel for the baby in that spider's web! Is it a diamond? It's so pretty. It sparkles and gleams and baby Jesus loves it, you can tell.'

Dorothy peered upwards. Miraculously, Charlie's web had caught one of Dorothy's snowflakes, a delicate, fragile crystal. And as Dorothy glanced at baby Jesus, she could almost have sworn he winked.

Another Resolution for Dorothy

Yet again, Dorothy's New Year resolution had gone by the board about ten minutes into January 1st. She had definitely intended to lose weight this New Year, but the desire had been a tad stronger than the will power, and she had succumbed to the first post-Christmas crumb she had spotted.

'After all,' she reasoned, 'one cannot allow the Christmas excess to go to waste,' completely failing to realise that thereby the Christmas excess would definitely go to waist.

By mid-January Dorothy was several ounces heavier, and for a little elderly mouse with short fat legs, that was a distinct disadvantage. She tried to scamper about the church floor to keep warm, but her fat little legs refused to comply. She attempted to climb onto a hassock to curl up in the warmth, but there was such creaking and groaning from her elderly joints that she was forced to abandon the effort.

Dorothy knew some of her more distant cousins hibernated all winter and she thought that was an excellent idea, but was only able to fall into a sort of induced torpor herself. She was, after all, a church mouse rather than a common field mouse, and as such had a certain status to maintain. She couldn't afford to sleep too deeply or for too long in case she missed something important. So Dorothy crept into her little nest under the tower and stayed there, as the only marginally warm place in the church except on Sundays, when the heating was on, but stayed a little alert. She didn't stay there all the time, though. She always ventured forth after the service on Sundays when everyone had departed, in the hope of a few residual biscuit crumbs, but pickings were usually scarce in winter.

She had discovered at the back of church a box containing items folk had brought for the Norwich Food Bank, but after investigation gave that up in disgust as everything was either in tins or strong packaging. Besides, as a good church mouse Dorothy's conscience wouldn't allow her to steal food from those who were so poor they needed help from Food Banks.

Apart from the extravagant post-Christmas pickings, Dorothy had little food throughout January, and February didn't look much better. It started with a church

Christmas meal at the White Horse, which meant no coffee—and more to the point, no biscuits—were served after the morning service.

By the end of February when she woke up properly, Dorothy discovered she was moving much more quickly and found she could climb better than she had for months. She looked at herself in wonder and realised she was now a lean, mean mouse, very ready for Spring.

'It's amazing,' she thought, 'how I worried about gaining weight after Christmas. I needn't have worried at all. God had it all in hand. It was just a question of waiting. Next year my resolution will be to stop worrying and leave life in God's hands. And I'll definitely do my best to keep that one!'

But as she laid her little grey head on her little grey paws in her patch of watery winter sunlight on the church floor, she had already forgotten all about resolutions.

Dorothy Loved Spring

Dorothy loved Spring. Not that she saw much of it being mostly confined to her home in the church, but she was very well aware that her patch of sunlight on the church floor was growing warmer and she could both see and smell the gorgeous, colourful flowers decorating the church.

But she didn't care to go outside. Charlie Spider had wisely informed her that she had a condition called 'agoraphobia', explaining that it meant an irrational fear of going outside, but since Dorothy couldn't even pronounce the word let alone worry her tiny brain over what it might mean, she preferred to curl up in her lovely patch of sunlight with her head on her paws and go to sleep. Who would want to go outside anyway, she reasoned, when they had this huge church to live in with all its creature comforts?

Dorothy remembered going outside a couple of times before. Once in early Spring a year or two back, and once in Winter to collect snow, but that was to keep baby Jesus warm in his cradle at Christmas. And when there was just white snow outside, there was nothing to trouble Dorothy's senses. Spring was different. She had a vague memory of her earlier venture forth, full of light and colour and scent, but now she felt there were so many new and overwhelming sights and sounds that her head felt as though it might explode. So she stayed indoors. It was safer that way, and anyway, her legs felt as though they might not carry her. Why put yourself at risk by trying something new if you don't have to?

And yet, and yet…

Dorothy was aware that she might just possibly be missing out. There was a slight yearning inside her which seemed to grow and grow as soon as she had acknowledged it, and she couldn't find any way of calming it. If only she could return to the way things used to be, without any of these strange and uncomfortable feelings. Time was so good when she thought only of crumbs, sleep and the occasional chat with her great friends Charlie and Hercules. Why change the habits of a lifetime or face prospective dangers when there was no need to do so?

Truth was, Dorothy was terrified. What's more, she was alone. Charlie and Hercules were great to chat to and pass the time of day, but spiders could hardly be classed as protectors or even companions in the big wide world outside. There was nobody to hold Dorothy's paw.

Then she suddenly remembered, which was quite something for a mouse of very little brain. In the middle of May came Whitsun—or Pentecost as the Church insisted on calling it now—when Jesus' friends had been huddled together terrified that they might be next for the chop, but God had poured his very own spirit into them and their fear disappeared like magic.

Could that happen to me, thought Dorothy? Could—would—God take away my fear?

On Whit Sunday in the middle of May, Dorothy took a deep breath and said a prayer. 'Please God, can I have some of your spirit too? I'm only a little mouse so I wouldn't need much, but I do need help.'

She immediately felt better, and when the big church door opened to let the people in, Dorothy summoned all her new found courage and crept to the door. She looked out. She placed one tentative paw outside the door, then another and another and another until she found herself standing outside in the church yard, not too far from the door and not moving any further forward, but outside nonetheless. She breathed in the scent of the flowers, she revelled in the sunshine and the blue sky, she gazed in wonder at the trees, she listened to the song of the birds. And she marvelled. Her fat little legs were trembling and her elegant whiskers quivering and her fear was still there, but it was a little more muted. Suddenly it seemed like Spring with its new life had brought her hope.

Dorothy was so glad she had remembered Christianity was a religion about taking risks, because Jesus and new life and resurrection had reminded her that help was always available.

Is it a joke?

Dorothy had never understood the concept of jokes. It seemed to her that when anyone said something, you should take it at its face value. Her little mouse brain was incapable of sifting beneath the layers to unearth any hidden meaning beneath the words. Besides, that seemed to her to be a waste of time and effort. Why not say exactly what you meant and be done with it? Then everyone would understand and there would be no no room for any confusion. Dorothy had suffered from confusion many times, and was suffering again just now.

'Is it a joke? It is a joke, isn't it? One of those strange things humans laugh at?' Dorothy asked plaintively. She was really puzzled this time. Her tiny mouse brain always had difficulty working out what was funny and what wasn't. She had huge trouble computing human ideas of humour.

Charlie chuckled. As a spider of wisdom, she had no such trouble. She slid a mite further down her long silken thread hanging from the rafters, until she was just above Dorothy's little pink ear. 'It isn't supposed to be a joke,' she explained, 'but it is quite funny.'

Dorothy was even more confused. 'Funny? How can it be funny but not be a joke?'

'I suppose,' said Charlie Spider, who Dorothy acknowledged was the fount of all wisdom but now began to doubt that she knew absolutely everything, 'I suppose it's just one of those weird things human beings laugh at.'

Dorothy settled more comfortably into her patch of sunlight on the church floor. She still didn't understand. 'Yes, but why have Ash Wednesday—that day when human beings are full of misery and remorse for all their sins—on the same day as Valentine's Day when everyone is full of love and happiness? It's just weird, isn't it? And then to have Easter Day on April Fool's Day, well, that's ridiculous. Even I, a mouse of very little brain, can see that. After all, none of those times were funny, were they? I mean, Ash Wednesday and Easter Day are quite serious times for human beings, aren't they?' It was a long speech for Dorothy, and hence required considerable effort.

Charlie laughed. "Not quite such a little brain, Dorothy, if you've remembered those two important church dates and tied them into the human calendar! I think the prob-

lem is with the date of Easter. You see, Easter Sunday is always the Sunday following the first full moon after the 20th March, and that can vary by as much as a
month. Don't ask me why that should be because I don't know. And I agree, it's definitely odd. Very odd. But then, human beings are odd, aren't they? It was all set up
centuries ago in olden times when I suppose the moon was more important for sea-
sons and things than it is now, and it's never been changed. So it's just coincidence
that occasionally the most important festival of the Christian year should fall on 1st
April, April Fool's Day, and the day of repentance—Ash Wednesday, marking the
beginning of the six weeks of Lent which lead up to Easter—should fall on Valentine's Day. It doesn't happen very often. Do you see now?'

But with experience of Charlie's somewhat long and involved lectures, Dorothy had
fallen asleep ten minutes ago with her head on her tiny paws, her fat little legs
tucked underneath her and her tail comfortably encircling her fat little body. She
dreamed of summer and sunshine and warmth. She knew that Easter Day meant
Jesus had shown the world that death wasn't the end but that life went on in a different way, and that was enough for her. And she supposed that even human beings
knew that was no joke, whatever the date.

Dorothy Hears The News

Dorothy seldom paid any attention to the news since it rarely concerned her. When she did happen to overhear the occasional whisper, mostly it seemed to be about human beings deploring the state of the world and therefore of no consequence to Dorothy.

But on this particular occasion, the news sent shockwaves throughout Dorothy's small body, causing her whiskers to quiver and her little pink nose to twitch unbearably. She had spotted a lost smart phone lying on the church floor. Not quite knowing what it was, filled with curiosity, and rather hoping a recalcitrant crumb might appear on its surface, Dorothy tentatively placed a paw onto this strange, rectangular object. Immediately it lit up and a headline appeared: BBC News - Church Cats. Not that Dorothy could read, (that would be ridiculous, everyone knows mice can't read) but a voice on the phone apparently called Siri helpfully shouted the words out for her.

Church cats—what could it mean? As far as Dorothy knew, there was no such creature as a church cat. Mice had the monopoly on official church positions—or so she had always thought. Dorothy was terrified. Even though the phone refused to read out to her any of the words below the headline and sulkily switched off its light as soon as Dorothy removed her paw, she feared there was only one reason any church would harbour a cat—in order to catch mice.

Did it mean every church? Was this terrible news telling that her very own church here in Trowse was going to employ a cat with the sole purpose of catching her? Surely not! Surely the good Christian folk of St. Andrew's knew her well enough by now to realise that she threatened nobody, and indeed, played her own little part in keeping the church clean by gobbling up as many escaped crumbs as she could.

Nonetheless, Dorothy was worried. She couldn't get that headline out of her head, and when she should have been sleeping in her little patch of sunlight on the church floor, she lay awake with the words 'church cat' spinning round and round and round inside her head. And with every revolution the headline seemed to grow louder and more terrifying until Dorothy was a shivering mouse wreck. She tried to pray, but it was impossible. The headline drowned out every other thought.

She was so anxious that she froze when the church door opened. Perhaps this was the frightful moment when an alien cat would be set loose in the church. Where could Dorothy hide then? It was a well-known fact that cats could sniff out any hidden rodent and could spot the slightest hint of movement, so there would be no escape for a fat little elderly mouse.

But there was no miaow and no scampering of fleet cat paws on the stone floor. Instead a voice called out, 'I must have dropped it in here. I haven't been anywhere else. Hope I find it. There's a lot of rubbish on it, but it contains my life! My diary, my calendar, all my contacts….' Followed by in tones of deep relief, 'Oh look! There it is. Thank goodness.'

With that the phone was picked up and the voice said, 'Oh look! It's opened on Facebook, BBC News. Look, it's all about cats - church cats, sports cats, political cats. It's called Whiskers in the Workplace - Cats with Careers, felines who earn their keep. I told you there was a load of rubbish on it, although you'd think the BBC would be above this sort of thing. I can't believe what they peddle as news these days. I suppose they can't think of anything else to say. Anyway, it's nothing to do with us, here in Trowse. We don't have cats of any sort, thank goodness.'

And as Dorothy lay, still stupefied, footsteps clattered across the church floor, the door was opened and closed again, and the phone was gone forever.

As she managed to get up to stagger across to her little home under the tower, Dorothy breathed a sigh of relief and wondered why yet again she had spent a miserable half hour because she had forgotten to trust in the God who cared for her and for all human beings, all of the time. If only, she thought, I could remember to leave my life in God's hands. Then my unnecessary fears really would disappear for good.

Clearing The Cobwebs

Dorothy was in a panic. Ted the verger had taken out the long-handled brush from under the tower and was preparing to attack the church's cobwebs. Dorothy was desperate to warn her friend Charlie, and had visions of Charlie being swept away with the cobwebs.

Dorothy scuttled as fast as her fat little legs would carry her, to her patch on sunlight on the church floor, praying that Charlie would see her and climb down her silken thread so that Dorothy could warn her of the impending danger. Instead of lying down in her patch as she usually did, Dorothy hopped and jigged about in a frenzy, hoping against hope to attract Charlie's attention and squeaking as loud as her tiny mouse voice would allow. But nothing happened. Charlie failed to appear, the cobwebs were duly swept away and the brush returned to its post under the tower.

Dorothy stayed as long as she could gazing up towards the roof, but there was no sign of Charlie. Eventually Dorothy gave up and crept back to her own little home under the tower, full of anxiety about Charlie.

Next day when the church was empty, Dorothy ventured forth again and tried to call to Charlie, but despite her best efforts still she could only manage a tiny mouse-like squeak which didn't produce any results. Dorothy's anxiety increased. Where was Charlie? What had happened to her?

By the end of the week with no sign of Charlie, Dorothy was frantic. She forgot a bit over the weekend when the church was occupied again—it was always entertaining to watch the people in church, and there were always crumbs to be had—but by the beginning of the next week, convinced that Charlie had perished with the cobwebs, Dorothy entered a deep depression. Without Charlie, she felt so very alone.

She railed against God. 'Why couldn't you look after Charlie? Why didn't you protect her or at least warn her when there was danger? How can you be a God of love and not care about Charlie?'

Dorothy's faith began to waver. A fat tear rolled down her cheek as she dragged herself to her patch of sunlight. Life didn't seem worth living any more without Charlie. Besides, Dorothy thought to herself, if she no longer believed in God, would she have to move out from the church? Would she have to become one of those common field mice? The tears began to flow faster.

Then a laughing voice penetrated her mind. 'You're such a silly, Dorothy! This Is spring-cleaning time. Don't you remember that the church is always thoroughly brushed and polished after the winter grime? But my home is right up in the rafters, far too high for any brush. No brush can reach up there, however long its handle! And you won't have to move, no matter what you think about God. Don't you know that even people in church doubt God from time to time? That's what faith is - clinging onto God even when you're not sure of God's existence. God always comes right in the end. You just have to hang on in there.'

'Charlie!' Dorothy was so overjoyed she cried even harder. 'I thought you'd died! Where have you been all week?'

Charlie shrugged as best a spider with eight legs can shrug. 'Having a quiet time,' she said. 'Sometimes I just need to get away from it all. You should try it, Dorothy. It's a great remedy for anxiety.'

But Dorothy had already curled up in her patch of sunlight, folded her front paws over her little pink ears, twitched her little pink nose, and fallen fast asleep.

Dorothy Loved Weddings

Dorothy loved weddings, and by July the wedding season was in full swing. Dorothy loved the fashions worn by the guests, but she loved the wedding dress and the bridesmaids' dresses even more. And when the groom and other male members of the wedding party had matching cravats, she was in seventh heaven, feasting her eyes on the glitter and glamour.

But there was more than that. The church was filled with joy and laughter, so that nobody noticed a plump elderly mouse stealthily creeping around, wrinkling her little pink nose to absorb the scent of the beautiful flower arrangements, and pricking her tiny ears to catch every nuance of the music, words and laughter.

There were never any crumbs after a wedding since the guests generally departed elsewhere for the wedding feast, but people tended to hang about for quite a long time for myriads of photographs. Dorothy did her best to inch her way into as many of the photos as she could, but since feet didn't feature greatly in the photographer's focus, she was seldom spotted.

But Dorothy was puzzled. She asked Charlie, that fount of all knowledge, 'Why is it, when weddings are such happy occasions and the bride and groom clearly love each other very much, that so many marriages end in separation or divorce? How does that unhappiness creep in? I shall never understand humans!'

Charlie explained, 'Weddings are very romantic, but life is less so. If the couple can't move out of the romance phase, things tend to fall apart.'

'What's romance?' Dorothy asked.

Charlie sighed. There were times when Dorothy's naivety was unbelievably irritating. 'Romance is kind of like living in a fairy tale. Everything is wonderful and the beloved can do no wrong. But at the end of a long, hard day, when they're both tired and have to start cooking meals or doing housework, they can get snappy with each other. And if they haven't learned how to forgive or how to apologise, things can go badly wrong. And sometimes it's worse when they produce babies, because then they don't get any sleep at all and they start to scream at each other. Sometimes, not always,' she hastened to add. She didn't want to give Dorothy entirely the wrong idea about human nuptials.

'I see,' said Dorothy. Her brow wrinkled, she thought for a moment, because her elderly mouse brain didn't work quite as quickly as it once had. Then she said, 'So I guess that's why they get married in church. Because church helps with love and forgiveness and all that stuff. And God is always there for them, to help them whenever they need help. No wonder I love church weddings!'

And she curled up in her little patch of sunlight on the church floor and fell asleep, dreaming of confetti and wedding cake.

Dorothy Is Outraged

Dorothy was outraged. When the big oak door at the back of church had opened, a strange mouse had crept inside. Dorothy drew herself up on her fat little legs and prepared to do battle. How dare strange field mice sneak into her domain?

Alert for the first signs of her crumbs being stolen, Dorothy was ready to pounce. But to her surprise, the strange mouse crept into Dorothy's patch of sunlight on the church floor and curled up, making no attempt to forage. Still, that would never do. It was Dorothy's patch, and she wasn't about to allow anyone else to sleep there.

Whiskers bristling, she wobbled over to the errant mouse as fast as her stout little body would allow. It was less formidable than she had intended, but she made up for it with a loud voice. It came out as a loud squeak, but at least it woke the stranger.

'What are you doing here?' Dorothy demanded. 'This is my church. No field mice or town mice are allowed in here. It's my home and all those crumbs you can see belong to me. What's more,' she added, building up a steam of righteous indignation, 'you're lying in my patch of sunlight.'

The strange mouse sleepily held out a paw. 'Pleased to meet you,' he said. 'I'm Alfaar, the mosque mouse. I popped in for a few minutes because I'm so tired. As it's Ramadan I haven't eaten since before dawn, and that was at 3.30 this morning.'

Dorothy was immediately contrite. 'You can sleep in my patch as long as you like then,' she conceded, 'and have some of my crumbs,' she added generously. Alfaar sighed, resting his head on his paws. Dorothy noticed that he was actually quite handsome, with his sleek brown fur and deep brown eyes, although sadly much younger than Dorothy.

He said, 'That's kind of you, but during Ramadan all we Muslims must fast from before dawn until after sunset.'

'But that's,' Dorothy wrinkled her little pink nose, trying to work out the sums, 'nearly eighteen hours, isn't it?' She was alarmed at the prospect of no food during all that time. 'Why on earth do you do that?'

'It's to commemorate the first revelation of the Quran - our holy book - to the prophet Muhammad (blessings be upon him.) It's a month of prayer and fasting and doing charitable acts. It's very good self-discipline,' he added, with a sideways glance at Dorothy's slightly overweight frame.

Dorothy blinked. 'A whole month with almost no food?' Then not wanting to be rude, she added, 'It's really good to meet you, Alfaar. You seem to be just like me, even though you have a different religion. Stay as long as you like, and I do hope you come again.'

'Well,' said Alfaar, 'thank you. After all, we worship the same God, even though we Muslims call him Allah. But we're all mice, the same as each other beneath the surface.'

'Hm,' said Dorothy thoughtfully, pictures of luscious crumbs and that uncomfortable word, 'self-discipline' filling her mind. 'I think I'll stay as a church mouse rather than a mosque mouse, if it's all the same to you.'

Dorothy's Birthday

Dorothy was mega-excited, because August was her birthday month. At least, she had decided that August would be her birthday month, although she had no idea what 'birthday' actually meant.

'I've heard all the people singing 'Happy Birthday' at the end of the Sunday morning service loads of times,' she informed Charlie, who was hanging on a silken thread all the way from the rafters. 'And everyone gets really excited and claps and there's a lot of laughter. But best of all, there's usually cake after the service and cake means crumbs. So I think I'm going to have a birthday this month.'

Charlie sighed. 'Do you know what a birthday is?'

'Well, not exactly. No. But it definitely involves cake and—'

'—cake means crumbs. Yes, I know. ' Charlie frowned. 'But you can't just pick any old month and decide it's your birthday. Your birthday has to be the anniversary of the date you were born.'

Dorothy was confused. 'But I don't remember the date I was born. I was too tiny to remember anything and anyway, it was a very long time ago. How can I possibly know?'

Charlie shrugged, which was quite difficult for a spider with eight legs. They all had to work in unison. 'If you can't remember the date, I'm afraid you can't celebrate your birthday.'

Dorothy gazed up at her friend in dismay. A fat tear rolled down her cheek and her lip quivered. ' I can't have a birthday? No cake? That's not fair!' Then she had a thought. 'Im sure I once heard that the Queen has two birthdays. Could I borrow one of hers?'

Charlie said, 'She has her own birthday which she celebrates with her own family, then she has an official birthday so that the whole nation can celebrate. There's a special event in London called 'Trooping The Colour,' when lots of soldiers parade in their bright uniforms and it's a splendid spectacle.'

Dorothy brightened up immediately. 'Then I'll have an official birthday too! I don't need any soldiers or any spectacles, just cake. Anyway, I don't wear glasses.' Then she had another thought. 'Does God have a birthday?'

Unsure how to answer this, Charlie began to climb up the silken thread back to her home in the rafters. Then she had a brainwave. 'Jesus had a birthday,' she called down. 'On Christmas Day. That's why we celebrate Christmas and give each other presents. And that's why we make our own birthdays special too.'

Dorothy said, 'So Jesus was born on Christmas Day?'

Charlie squirmed. This conversation was becoming unsettling but she felt obliged to tell the truth. 'Not exactly. No one knows exactly when Jesus was born, so the Christian Church chose December 25th to celebrate his birthday. It brightens up the long, cold months of winter.'

Dorothy beamed. 'That's alright, then. I shall be like Jesus but celebrate my birthday in August to brighten up the summer. There will be cake, won't there?'

And she scampered across the church floor as fast as her fat little legs would carry her, her head full of thoughts of her very first birthday with cake - even though she was really quite old.

Dorothy Is Confused

Dorothy found herself confused when September came at last. She was confused because the summer had been so hot that she had abandoned her spot in the sun on the church floor and crept nearer to the big church door, where occasionally a breeze would slide underneath to fan her sweltering fur. And she had felt so tired and lethargic all summer long that she had been hardly able to summon the energy to forage for crumbs, and that was very unlike her.

Charlie, that fount of (almost) all knowledge, had loftily informed Dorothy that the hot weather was down to 'global warming' and 'climate change', and started on one of her long lectures on the subject. Dorothy had no idea what any of it meant, and she didn't much care, either. Climate change! All she wanted was a temperature that was neither too hot nor too cold, where she could feel like her old self again and actually move without too much discomfort.

The other thing that had confused her was that the annual Harvest Festival service, held to thank God for the harvest safely gathered in for another year, was no longer on the last Sunday in September or even the first Sunday in October, but was now right at the beginning of September. It didn't feel right to Dorothy. She really didn't like all this sudden and upsetting change. Charlie informed her that for years now the harvest had been gathered in at least a month earlier than in former times—because of climate change. And this year the weather was so hot that the harvest was mostly finished in July, so Dorothy thought maybe it did make a bit of sense after all.

But she was troubled. Quite apart from the delicious harvest lunch after the service, Harvest Festival brought all sorts of delights for a church mouse. There was the sheaf of corn by the choir stalls, where nobody noticed the odd morsel disappearing into a hungry mouse, the wheelbarrow so beautifully decorated with so many different vegetables that some overflowed towards the floor and a waiting Dorothy, and the fine harvest loaf on the high altar, which responded well to the occasional nibble. Dorothy was used to storing grains of wheat and a few nuts and (of course) crumbs, to tide her through the winter until the church put on some other feast. Now she wondered whether her store would last for a whole extra month.

She said a little prayer for help and guidance, half expecting God to somehow forbid her to forage for food from the harvest display, but the very next Sunday heard folk talking about a '90th birthday celebration' and a 'christening with food afterwards' and she knew then that she'd be OK. There was extra food to come during September.

'Thank you God for Harvest Festival and all other events that include food,' she whispered, as her fat little legs carried her to her home under the tower.

Dorothy Dreads The Winter

It was definitely Autumn. Although she rarely ventured outside, and never in anything like cold weather, Dorothy knew it was Autumn. Living inside the church for the whole of her life, she was unable to see the leaves changing colour or falling from the trees, but still she knew it was Autumn. The weekly flower arrangements in church had subtly altered, with fewer bright colours but more muted shades of brown and orange with the occasional splash of pink. And already it was much colder in church. Gone were those stifling days of summer (which she could hardly remember, having the memory span of an elderly goldfish) when she would search for any cool spot she could find. Now, she again sought out her patch of sunlight on the church floor whenever she could, and when there was no sun, Dorothy would curl up in her little nest under the tower, struggling to keep warm.

Of course, as in any life-changes, there were compensations. In Dorothy's view, they mainly concerned food, which was plentiful in church in Autumn, for there were many events to mark special times in the church's year. In September there had been Harvest Festival (many stray crumbs under the tables), a 90th birthday party (more stray crumbs, which this time were delicious cake crumbs) and a church family baptism (even more stray crumbs, which naturally required a home in Dorothy's stomach.) And it was so good to see lots of people in church. Although Dorothy rarely ventured out among them, she liked to see the people and hear the friendly chatter.

But even Dorothy knew that Autumn meant Winter was rapidly approaching, and she rather dreaded it. She was feeling her age, and with the onset of cold and rain her fat little legs felt as if they could barely carry her. Her joints creaked and groaned, and she was often in pain. Not that she grumbled about it. There was only Charlie and occasionally Charlie's son Hercules where she could offload her groans, and since they were both acrobatic spiders shinning with ease up and down their silken threads hanging from the rafters, they could never understand.

'I wish God would take this pain away,' she thought. 'Jesus healed so many people in his day, why can't he heal me today?'

Then, in a rare moment of clarity, she had a brief memory of last winter. It hadn't been as bad as she had anticipated, and hey! She was still here to tell the tale. She had survived it.

'Hm,' thought Dorothy. 'Perhaps that's it. Perhaps God gives us lots of compensation for things that happen to us (if only we can see the compensation). Perhaps God doesn't take away our pain, at least, not when we want, but perhaps God helps us through to the other side of it. Yes, maybe that's part of the message of Christianity. That God gives us strength and sees us through.'

And she curled up in her little patch of sunlight on the church floor, determined to try out her theory on Charlie, who knew everything. That is, unless she forgot.

Dorothy's Christmas Scare

It was not that Dorothy disliked Christmas. On the contrary, all year round she looked forward to that time of fun and laughter, sparkly lights and decorations and of course, good food. But just at the moment, with her little fat legs tangled up in tinsel which had inadvertently dropped from the big church Christmas tree, and her mouth too full of bits of stale biscuit which had once been a decoration for the tree, she wished Christmas was over and done.

How was she to know the enticing-looking biscuits in the shape of Christmas trees or stars or angels were last year's ornaments and well past their sell-by date? But with a mouth so full she was unable to chew, and legs in a tangle, Dorothy was stuck. No matter how much she writhed and wriggled, she was unable to free her legs from the tinsel, and she could neither swallow the revolting stale biscuit nor remove it from her mouth in the sort of genteel fashion suitable to a church mouse.

Dorothy tried to call for help, but there was no help forthcoming. Besides, Charlie and her big son Hercules were the only other residents in the church as far as Dorothy knew, and she thought it unlikely a couple of spiders could help very much. Charlie and Hercules might be good at spinning webs, but were considerably less adept at unspinning.

When the church doors opened on Christmas Eve and folk began to pour in for the Christingle Service, Dorothy began to panic. If she was spotted, the churchwardens might be tempted to set a trap for her and if they laced it with tasty cheese, Dorothy knew she would be unable to resist. But worse than that, all human beings had such big feet. If she couldn't get out of the way, Dorothy was terrified of being crushed underfoot.

Dorothy risked a glance at the Christmas stable. She sent a hurried prayer to the baby in the manger, 'Please help me!' without any confidence that her prayer would be heard, given that this baby Jesus was only a tiny doll.

At that moment a huge human foot was raised above her and Dorothy cringed, sure that her end had come. But amazingly, the foot landed on the trail of tinsel, holding it so firm that Dorothy found she could actually move. As she began to scamper away as fast as her fat little legs would carry her, the tinsel unwound itself from her legs and with her heart beating in double quick motion, she made it to her home under the tower. There she was able to discreetly remove the contents of her mouth.

And suddenly, everything was OK. 'Christmas is great after all,' Dorothy sighed happily. 'I'm so glad Jesus was born and that he can still work miracles today— even at those times when he's only a tiny doll!'

Charlie's News

'Have you heard?' Charlie Spider had shimmied down her silken thread from the rafters and was whispering in Dorothy's ear.

Dorothy twisted a little so that her good ear was towards Charlie. Dorothy was finding it slightly more difficult to pick up Charlie's sibilant murmur these days. If only Charlie would stop mumbling!

'Heard what? I haven't heard anything for weeks!' Dorothy's reply was a gentle reproof reminding Charlie that it was some time since she had bothered to approach her friend.

Charlie ignored the implied criticism. 'My home up in the roof nearly got very wet,' she spluttered indignantly.

'What?' Dorothy was immediately contrite, and worried for her friend. 'How? Why? What happened?' Then she added with a frown, 'How do you mean, you nearly got wet? Surely you were either wet or dry?'

But Charlie was too full of her story to notice the remonstrance. 'It was somewhere around Christmas, I'm not sure exactly when. I heard this noise on the roof, quiet at first but then footsteps stomping around and it sounded like something being pried up from the roof. It was really terrifying. I thought about ghosts and things like the roof gargoyles coming to life. Silly, I know, but when it's dark these silly things tend to pop into your head. You wouldn't give them a second thought in daylight. Anyway, I found out later that some scumbags had stolen lead from the church roof. Good thing it was spotted before any heavy rain, otherwise my home would have been completely washed out and the church would have had loads of water damage.'

'Oh dear, that's terrible. I'm so sorry to hear that,' Dorothy said. But her mind was working quite well today. 'Hang on a minute, though. I thought you told me there were cameras and an alarm on the roof now?'

Charlie nodded as best a spider could. 'That's right, but some idiot had placed the camera near the edge of the roof where a drainpipe meets it. Apparently the thieves managed to climb the drainpipe and cover the camera with a bag. It won't happen again though, because they've moved the camera now to where no-one can get at it.'

'Hm,' Dorothy was thoughtful. 'So if the roof is damaged, who pays for the repairs?'

'The church people of course! I mean, I think they have insurance, but I heard someone mutter that it only pays part of the cost because so many churches are losing lead to thieves these days. And it'll be a hefty sum, what with lead being so expensive and all the architects and repair people and whatnot who've been up on the roof since.'

'Why do they use lead, then?' Dorothy murmured, intelligently, she thought.

'They have to. The church authorities won't allow them to use anything else. Something to do with history, I think,' she added, vaguely.

'It never rains but it pours!' Dorothy murmured, appropriately. Then she brightened. Since it hadn't rained since the lead was stolen, the church was still dry, her patch of sunlight on the church floor was safe, Charlie's home was intact, and perhaps there would be even more events in church (producing plenty of crumbs since food was always involved in church events) to raise money to repair the roof.

Clearly God was still in his heaven and everything was still (relatively) all right with the world, or at least, in the church.

Dorothy's Anxiety

Dorothy was very anxious. Of course, as her friend Charlie frequently remarked, if she didn't have something to worry about, she'd find something. But this was different. There was a lot of activity going on in church and it felt like things were changing.

Dorothy didn't like change. It made her feel uneasy, as though everything she had ever known and loved was falling away from her.

'Sing a song,' Charlie suggested, 'or do a little dance. That always helps.'

So Dorothy tried twerking. Not that she really knew what she was doing, but she had heard it involved wriggling your bum, and she thought it was probably the only dance she could manage, with her little fat legs and her stiff, elderly body. But when she heard Charlie shaking with laughter, she gave up. It hadn't helped, anyway. Dancing with four legs was nearly impossible, and she wondered how Charlie, with eight legs, knew anything at all about dancing. Anyway, she still felt anxious.

'There's something afoot,' she told Charlie, who looked down at her own eight legs and frowned. Something afoot for a spider sounded eight times serious.

'No,' Dorothy said. 'I don't mean there's anything wrong with your legs, or mine for that matter. But there's something going on in church. Everything's changing, and I don't like it. I think I might have to hide myself away where no one can see me. And if I cover my eyes, perhaps whatever it is that's upsetting me will disappear.'

So she crept inside a bag she spotted on the church floor, snuggled down right at the bottom, and soon began to snore.

***

Dorothy was so comfortable that it was many hours—and possibly several days—later that she awoke. She stretched and yawned and eased her way out of the bag, which was quite difficult since the twerking had made her joints unbearably stiff. Then she stopped in horror. The church had completely changed! There was no patch of sunlight on the church floor, and no little home under the tower. No lovely, comfortable, warm red chairs, no red carpet down the aisle. Instead, hard wooden pews.Worse, there was no sign of Charlie.

Even Dorothy with her tiny mouse brain soon realised this was an entirely different church. And when Dorothy heard some people speaking in a very strange accent, she nearly died. Then she heard the words, 'Welcome!' and 'We're so glad to see you here in Northumberland. We hope you'll be very happy here,' and she didn't feel quite so bad. This was a different church in a different part of the country, but hey! Dorothy was a church mouse, so perhaps she could fit in anywhere. Couldn't she? Could she find a new home here?

And with that she remembered that God was always around, supporting her and holding her and giving her strength, so perhaps the surroundings didn't matter quite as much as she had thought.

Dorothy twitched her little pink nose, flicked her long brown tail, and set about making herself a new home in a new place. But she knew she'd never forget Charlie, and vowed to send letters home to Charlie just as soon as she could.

Dorothy Writes A Letter

Somewhere up in the frozen North.

Dearest Charlie,

It seems so long since I saw you that I'm having to write now in case I forget what you look like. I don't think I will, but you know what my memory's like, especially these days. Now I'm getting older I find it more and more difficult to remember names, and faces aren't far behind either. But Marcus helps.

Marcus? Oh, he's like you only much bigger, about the size of a dinner plate. Everyone seems bigger up here, but that may be my faulty memory again. But back to Marcus. He has eight legs, just like you, and he lives somewhere in the church hidden away. I haven't quite found his home yet, as he just appears on a long silken thread from the roof, like you used to do. He's friendly though, and he told me there is this vast spiders' web which covers the whole world, well, practically the whole world. It's called the World Wide Web, or www for short. Then—according to Marcus—you just put in some sort of address, and your letter reaches the right place. And he seems to know all about other churches, and even about you. So on his instructions, I put in www.trowsechurch.co.uk, passed it over to Marcus and I hope and pray my letter reaches you. Actually, Marcus wrote it all for me. As he has eight legs like you, there are spare ones to write letters. I need all my four just to balance. Anyway, as you know, I can't read or write because I'm only a mouse.

Oh, I should have told you. You know the bag I crawled into which somehow magically transported me all these miles away? Well, I made it my temporary home for a while. Temporary because as you know I'm a church mouse, so when the bag (and its owner) found their way to a church, I crept out and hid. Until I find my bearings I can't tell you much about where I am, because I don't really know. I do miss you though. It's quite lonely with only Marcus for occasional company. I say occasional because as soon as he was spotted, for some strange reason there was a hue and cry in church and someone fished out an electric spider catcher. Marcus only just shot up his silken thread in time. Even so, they destroyed his thread so he'll have to weave a new one to find me again.

I don't know when that will be because I'm reluctant to crawl out of my space just yet on account of the fact that my fat little legs may never be able to find their way back in. I need to find my own little home here in this new church. I don't want to lose my status. I had already managed to find quite a bit of delicious food in here, as the church serves coffee and biscuits after the morning service, and prior to that, the bag's owner seemed to have a diet consisting almost entirely of chocolate. I didn't mind. The crumbs were exceedingly tasty until they melted and stuck to my fur. That wasn't quite so good. But I spent all day licking it off.

Oops! My little pink ears are suddenly pricking and my whiskers are twitching, a sure sign someone is coming. So I need to hide away.

God bless you, Charlie. You made my life so special and I thank God for you every day.

Until next time,

With love, your very own Dorothy. Xxx

Dorothy's New Home

Dorothy wasn't sure what to make of her new home. In a way it was exciting, exploring a new church and deciding where she would make her little nest, hidden from human eyes, but in another way it was scary and daunting. She was so relieved that she had met up with Marcus who had been friendly and encouraging, but she very much missed Charlie. Charlie had always been there, and as the fount of (almost) all wisdom, could answer nearly all of Dorothy's questions and reassure her when things didn't go quite according to plan. Dorothy was a bit chary of expecting Marcus to fulfil that role in quite the same way. She didn't want to demand so much of him that he scuttled away in fright, and Dorothy felt she shouldn't rely on him too much. After all, she scarcely knew him yet, and since she didn't know his habits, he might easily disappear at any moment.

So Dorothy set about exploring her new church. She hoped there were no other mice in residence, leaving plenty of scope for Dorothy to become the first church mouse of St. Mary the Virgin (the church, not the person.) In many ways it was similar to St. Andrew's, but in other ways quite different. There seemed to be more space and Dorothy especially loved the Children's Corner, which was wide and comfortable and warm. And since coffee and biscuits were served there after the service, there were usually rich pickings for a little, elderly overweight mouse.

The wooden pews were much less comfortable and less welcoming than the lovely warm chairs at St. Andrew's, but Dorothy spied a soft blanket draped over many of the pews for anyone who felt cold. She assumed that included her when the church was devoid of human beings, and discovered the blankets, which were all alike in a lovely pale shade of purple were just as warm and soft as they looked. She also discovered embroidered pew cushions which she felt mitigated the hardness of the wood and were quite good burrowing places for a timid elderly mouse.

But warm and comfortable as it was, it wasn't a home such as Dorothy had been used to under the tower at St. Andrew's. She hunted about for a suitable spot, somewhere well out of the way and hidden, but with good access to the main body of the church. Perhaps the organ loft? Or the choir vestry?

Then Dorothy discovered the tower. It was a large, squat square tower with so much room beneath it that the space was filled with all sorts of oddments—a ladder, flower pedestals, much other clutter, and stairs leading up to the organ loft and the bells. Dorothy crept in to see whether she could make her new home under the tower just like her old home, but to her horror found evidence of other mice. Since they had left their droppings lying around, it was clear to Dorothy that they weren't church mice at all, but just vagabond strangers who were squatting. Dorothy resolved that her first task would be to rid the church of all other mice, for a church mouse would never leave droppings. Ugh! Disgusting. Dorothy wasn't at all sure how she would manage the eviction, but maybe Marcus could help. He probably didn't like squatters in his home any more than Dorothy did.

Anyway, plenty of time for that. Meanwhile, Dorothy searched along the skirting board until she found a suitable hole, right next to the central heating pipe and just under the organ loft, so warm and cosy. She squeezed in, and by carrying in morsels of old wool, scraps of felt and discarded paper, soon began to make a nest which felt very much like home.

'Thank you, God,' Dorothy whispered. 'I think this will do splendidly. I should have known you are always on my side, whatever happens, so thank you. I'll do my best to be a church mouse you can be proud of.'

And then, exhausted from her labours, she laid her little head on her little brown paws, folded her tail around herself, and fell fast asleep.

Dorothy Becomes A Bailiff

Dorothy hadn't much idea what to do about the mice-squatters, but being a spider and therefore highly intelligent and knowledgable, Marcus had plenty of ideas.

'First,' he said importantly, 'you need to entice them out into the churchyard and then—'

'—how will I do that?' Dorothy interrupted.

'—then,' continued Marcus, as though she hadn't spoken at all, 'you need to gather up all their belongings and throw them out. Meanwhile, I shall seal all the little holes with my purpose-spun webs so that they'll never get in again.'

'Oh!' said Dorothy, her mind struggling to catch up with Marcus' grand plan. Even she, with her tiny mouse brain, thought there might be one or two holes in it. 'You do know I never go outside the church, don't you? I'm too old for that sort of caper. Besides, it all sounds like a lot of hard work, dragging out all the nests and belongings. They'd be back before I'd finished. And what if I got stuck outside? How would I get back in myself?'

Marcus sniffed, a difficult manoeuvre for a spider without much in the way of a nose. 'if you don't want my help,' he said haughtily, and prepared to climb his silken thread again.

Dorothy said hastily, 'It's not that, Marcus. It's just that there's only one of me and I don't move very fast, these days. I think I'd need some help.'

'Hm. I see what you mean.' Marcus cast a somewhat derogatory glance at Dorothy's fat little legs and stout little body. 'What about if you get them outside and I manage to keep them there until you've finished the clearing out? Would that work?'

'Depends how long you can delay them,' Dorothy retorted, envisaging countless trips, laden with heavy belongings.

Marcus smiled mysteriously, attempting to tap the side of his non-existent nose with one of his eight legs. 'Leave that up to me. I'll sort it. I know a man (well, a male, anyway) who can help. Off you go, Dorothy. Find plenty of crumbs and leave a trail which they won't be able to help but follow.'

Dorothy sighed. She was pretty sure she could find enough crumbs, but with her agoraphobia was deeply anxious about venturing beyond the confines of the building. There was only one thing for it. She sent up a prayer—please help me, God—gritted her tiny pointed teeth and set to work.

In the end she managed it. No sooner had she laid the trail than the errant mice were greedily scampering after it, right out into the churchyard. Dorothy heaved a sigh of relief and scuttled back into the church as fast as her little fat legs would allow her.

It was while she was emptying nests and throwing out belongings that she was struck with a pang of conscience. Wasn't the church supposed to be a sanctuary which welcomed everyone and never turned anyone away? And when through the partially open door she glimpsed a large ginger cat chasing the squatter mice, she felt even worse. So that was Marcus' grand plan!

'I'm sorry, God,' whispered Dorothy. 'Perhaps we should've let them stay. After all, this is your house. I hope they don't get hurt.'

But she was so tired after her exertions that she rested her head on her little brown paws and fell fast asleep. When she awoke, Marcus was hanging around on his thread beside her.

'Welcome to your new job as official church mouse of St. Mary the Virgin,' he said grandly. 'And by the way, don't spare another thought for those squatters. They've all run off back to their own home where they belong. All shall be well and all shall be well and all manner of things shall be well.'

But Dorothy wasn't listening. She'd nodded off again in a patch of sunlight on what was now her very own church floor.

Dorothy Is Horrified

It had been several weeks now. Dorothy was becoming quite used to her new home, which was warm and cosy in the vestry under the organ loft. Now all the vagabond mice had been evicted never to return, life was much more comfortable for a little fat elderly church mouse, especially with a staunch ally like Marcus just a silken thread away. Dorothy was slowly growing more confident and had begun to venture out into the church at the end of the morning service, mostly so that she was in prime position to gather up biscuit crumbs as soon as possible.

This meant that she was in church when the notices were read out, and this is when she experienced a gigantic shock. To her horror, Dorothy heard that the church people were planning to put a toilet into the vestry under the tower. Not only planning, already they had permission from the church authorities to start the work, and apparently had even now raised sufficient funds to begin. She knew what that meant. Workmen and noise and dust and everything being cleared out, including her new home. Dorothy nearly wept. The church she had just left, St. Andrew's at Trowse in Norwich all those many miles away, was also planning to build a toilet under the tower just where Dorothy's old home had been. It seemed like too much of a coincidence. Did every church build a toilet under the tower or was Dorothy just unlucky?

'What about all those hours of work, clearing out those rogue mice and then building my own little home?' she complained to Marcus. 'It's not as though I ask for much. Just a little space to call my own and enough crumbs to keep body and soul together. And I look after the church keeping it free of crumbs and errant mice invaders. But what thanks do I get? I'm going to be chased out again, and then what will I do?'

'Hm.' Marcus always stalled for time, pretending he was thinking deeply when he had no idea of the answer. 'Hm.' He scratched his head with two of his eight legs to give added gravitas. Then his eyes brightened. 'There are human beings just like you,' he said. 'People who are forced out of their homes through war or stuff like that. They become refugees and go to live in refugee camps. You could do that.'

'What?' Dorothy was horrified. 'I'm a church mouse. I can't live just anywhere. It has to be in a church. Besides, I don't want to leave here now. Im just getting settled, and the people here are nice. They leave quite a lot of crumbs for me, and I've even found a patch of sunlight on the church floor. I can't move again. It would be too much.'

'No, you're quite right. I don't think it's a very good life for human refugees, actually. No work, not enough food or medicines, and lots of other human beings don't seem to want them around, strange as that might seem. Let's forget that as a possible solution. I think you'd better say a prayer and ask God for help.' Marcus breathed a sigh of relief. Shifting the problem onto God was the perfect fix. If everything went wrong God could be blamed, and if everything turned out well, Marcus could claim it was his brilliant idea of suggesting God's help in the first place.

So Dorothy said a prayer, not expecting much in the way of an answer. Why would God bother with a fat little mouse when there were all those human refugees needing so much more help? But she felt strangely calmer after her prayer, and decided to stay in her own little home for as long as possible, until she really was forced out. She could almost hear Charlie saying, 'No point in worrying this far in advance. Church things take ages to come to fruition. Wait until something actually happens. Then the answer will be there before you. You'll see.'

Dear Charlie. Dorothy missed her so much that she felt she had no option but to seek out her patch of sunlight on the church floor, rest her head on her little brown paws and sink into a deep sleep. Maybe, she thought sleepily, she would write to Charlie again just as soon as she woke up. Or maybe not.

Dorothy Writes Another Letter

Dearest Charlie,

I've been thinking about you a lot, lately. Marcus says it's called 'home-sickness' but I don't know what that means. I just know I miss you loads. Marcus also said you'd written to me, but I'm afraid I've never seen your letter. Marcus said it was lost in the ether because that's what happens to a lot of emails. I suppose it could be true, with all those millions of spiders just like you and Marcus running all over the World Wide Web delivering mail. Must be a tricky job.

Anyway, I wanted to tell you about life up here. Contrary to what everybody in Norfolk told me, I haven't noticed it being particularly cold up here. In fact we had some searingly hot days earlier in the summer, but that all seems to have disappeared now.

There aren't so many folk in church today because the schools are on holiday so the families (including the vicar and his family) are all away. Although actually I don't think that's the main reason there are so few here today. (Obviously I'm anxious because fewer people mean fewer crumbs, especially if there aren't any children.)

No, the real reason is that the weather has changed. It's been raining nearly all day every day for over a week now, some of it torrential. There have been bright periods in between and the occasional dry and sunny (although clammy) day, but it's been so wet that there are floods all over the place. Not that our church is ever likely to be flooded since it's built on a hill, but the access for some folk is across a bridge over the river Tyne. They park on the far side of the bridge then walk across, but today the car park is flooded and the lower end of the bridge is under water too, so nobody can get across.

I immediately thought of Trowse and wondered whether you have the same weather, Charlie? If so, I do hope you haven't had another flood inside the church, being so low lying and so close to the brook. I well remember the last flood only a few years ago, when those lovely red carpets had to be stripped up and the wooden floor repaired. And I do hope nobody else has stolen lead from the roof, because if so the roof will certainly be leaking.

Oh my, Charlie! What a lot of worries are involved with a church when the weather is bad! It's funny being in the church when there are so few folk around. I mean, I know the church is a building, but it feels much more as though it's people that make it what it is. I'm so glad I've found a welcoming church up here. At least, I've seen them warmly welcoming each other although most of them probably don't know I exist, so I'm not at all sure the welcome extends to me, even though I hoover up their crumbs on a regular basis. Still, Marcus is brilliant. He tells me all I need to know and like you used to do, he looks out for me. Also like you, he knows everything. Are all spiders super-intelligent?

It's great to have friends, even if it's only one good friend. But I suppose that's a lot of what church is about and why folk keep coming back—because they feel safe and loved among friends.

Charlie, I remember you telling me that's exactly what Jesus did. He was genuinely friendly with everyone no matter who they were, and that's why they loved him so much. So maybe a God-filled church is one where people (and fat little mice and eight-legged spiders) know they are loved.

Thank you, Charlie, for your friendship over so many years. Please keep in touch. I'll try and get Marcus to work harder at intercepting your letters and passing them on to me. After all, that's what friends do, isn't it? Look out for each other?

Until next time, keep safe and keep loving.

Your fat little friend,

Dorothy.

Further Correspondence from Dorothy

Somewhere up in the not-so-frozen North.

Dearest Charlie,

You'll never believe it, but it's been a thin summer for me. As you know, it's usually winter which is the thin time, but this year there have been few people in church over the summer, so the quantity of crumbs has dropped significantly. Not the quality, you understand. Crumbs here are delicious - and on one memorable occasion were from scones rather than biscuits - but there haven't been many of them.

After the flood which I told you about in my last letter, the bridge was closed for the whole of August for repairs. According to Marcus that meant there was only one other relatively easy route into the village, but unfortunately that road was closed for roadworks of some kind at exactly the same time! I know, you can hardly believe it, can you? The only other way to this church for anyone living outside the village needed a detour of several miles and about forty minutes, so it wasn't surprising that no one bothered to come.

That put paid to August, as far as church was concerned. But not only that, last Sunday there was a race on and all roads from the nearest village were closed for the runners. It reminded me of St. Andrew's when Norwich City Football Club plays at home, and there's absolutely nowhere to park. Do you remember Easer Day a few years ago? Norwich City was in the Premier Division then too, and church was half empty on what should have been the busiest day of the year. It made the chocolate pickings after the service sparse indeed.

Which reminds me. Any update on getting that common land next to the church for parking? That would solve all your problems and there would be crumbs galore for my successor, Daisy. Unfortunately Marcus doesn't think there are any easy solutions up here. Although it's unlikely the bridge will have to be repaired again for a few more years, we've had such torrential rain lately that the river is full to overflowing and there's a strong possibility the bottom end of the bridge will be flooded yet again.

Anyway Charlie dear, enough doom and gloom because next week is Harvest Festival, and you know how that makes my heart sing. Since it will be my first Harvest

Festival up here, I don't yet know whether it will be a good old-fashioned Harvest with sheaves of corn, a wonderful Harvest loaf and lots of fresh fruit and vegetables for me to nibble, or whether it will be what seems to be the modern trend of tinned and dried food. I hope not! Please pray for me, Charlie. Yes, I know I'm only an elderly overweight mouse with little fat legs, but I still have to eat, and I feel sure good Christian folk would never begrudge me a little of their surplus, just as they always give to any less fortunate than themselves, either here or in other countries.

I'm not sure what happens to the food after the Harvest service. I expect some of it goes to the local Food Bank and some to the local old folks' home, but with any luck (and some earnest prayers) I shall be able to harvest enough myself to keep me going for at least another month.

The other bit of good news is that so far, it feels quite warm in church. Not that we've reached the really cold weather yet, but the signs of church heat are promising. With my little nest under the tower, some good harvest food and enough warmth, I should be quite comfortable for a while yet.

Charlie, this may be my last letter for a while, but I should so love to hear from you. As you know, Marcus writes this down for me and he'll read out any correspondence from you, so do get going on that web thingy and send me your news.

With my love as always,

You little fat friend,

Dorothy.

Printed in Great Britain
by Amazon

87744231R00048